"You are no friend of Caesar if you

"Away with him! Crucify him!.. Giv

PILATE UNDER

PRESSURE 2

Sean Walsh

"I, Pontius Pilate, Governor of Judaea

by the gift of Caesar, will maintain

the Pax Romana at all costs… all costs."

A two-hander for the most part:

Pontius Pilate and Lucius, his C O

One scene where the person playing Lucius

becomes(!) Joseph of Arimathea. Optional.

'Can be performed on a conventionnel stage -

theatre, hall, church or In-The-Round,

in modern dress or as costume drama...

Introduction.

This is a powerful play based on Matthew's passion narrative, in particular on elements of Matthew's passion narrative that are unique to his gospel, such as the washing of hands by Pilate, his wife's warning –"Have nothing to do with this man," and the request of the Jewish authorities to place a guard on the tomb of Jesus.

The author has woven an engaging and thought provoking drama on the basis of these hints in the text of Matthew, filling out the gaps in the text in a dramatically satisfying way.

The title 'Pilate under Pressure' captures the essence of the drama.

Pilate: is portrayed as a man caught between his duty to Rome and his obligation to justice…

His dilemma is that of everyone caught between obligations to the institution one represents and loyalty to a greater truth which challenges that institution.

The dramatist draws the reader/viewer into this dilemma with great skill. It is a play that is worth reading, and in particular viewing, many times. It throws light on our own struggles to do what is right when it is easier to do otherwise.

- Martin Hogan.

Priest of the Dublin diocese

Lecturer in Sacred Scripture,

DCU. (rtd.)

ONE

LUCIUS: Good morning, Sir.

PILATE: Ah, Lucius... 'Up and about so early?

LUCIUS: I, I slept but fitfully, Sir.

PILATE: And I. The journey from the coast should have tired me. And yet I was restless through all the long hours of darkness. As was her ladyship...

LUCIUS: Sir, I should tell you -

PILATE: But now the sun is up, the air balmly, while the city still slumbers.

LUCIUS: Sir, I -

PILATE: See, Lucius. Below and about us. Jerusalem. Have you ever viewed a more peaceful vista?

LUCIUS: Well, no, Sir. Not, not since we departed Italy.

PILATE: Yet so much unrest down there - discontent, anger, railing against Rome - in the squares, the narrow streets, the squalid dwelling places...

LUCIUS: An unrest that is fermenting, Sir, even as we speak.

PILATE: What?

LUCIUS: The Jews are on the move, Sir. Crowds of them, con verging here - on the Praetorium.

PILATE: Oh?

LUCIUS: My intelligence is they are in contentious mood. 'Roused by their religious leaders.

PILATE: Oh, ye gods! And I in high hope of a peaceful sojourn.

LUCIUS: It would seem unlikely, Sir.

PILATE: Such a troublesome Race! What is it this time?

LUCIUS: The Rabbis - priests of the Temple - have a prisoner.

PILATE: Prisoner?

LUCIUS: One of their own. Jesus. 'Hails from the North. From Galilee.

PILATE: And?

LUCIUS: They would have you try him - they are intent on obtaining the death penalty.

PILATE: Why? What has the wretch done to warrant crucifixion?

LUCIUS: Magic. Sorcery. Leading the people astray. Disturber of the Peace. Incitement to revolt and rebellion...

PILATE: What? Against Rome?

LUCIUS: 'Claims to be their King.

PILATE: King? Of the Jews? Huh...

LUCIUS: Any moment now they will be at the gates of this fortress, clamouring for a hearing.

PILATE: Ah, but why the urgency?

LUCIUS: 'Hard to tell with the Jews, Sir - well nigh impossible to read their minds.

PILATE: Hmmm... Is there something here below the surface?.. Oh, very well. I will go down to them anon. Now leave me, Lucius. See to your garrison.

LUCIUS: Sir...

PILATE: Hmmm... What is afoot here?..
What hidden from the eye?...
A people apart, their ways not our ways...
Jesus, eh. Jesus... King of the Jews?.. King of the rabble, more like...
But if he is their King why would they want him done to death?..
Well... we shall see...
Of this they can be assured:
they will have nothing from me but Roman justice - and Roman order.
The Peace of the Empire is all.
I will not tolerate disorder, countenance disruption...
I, Pontius Pilate, Governor of Judaea by the gift of Caesar, will maintain the Pax Romana at all costs...
all costs.

TWO

PILATE: Yes, Lucius, what is it?

LUCIUS: Sir, your wife sends an urgent warning -

PILATE: Warning?

LUCIUS: You are to have nothing to do with this man. Last night she dreamt she suffered much on his account.

PILATE: She said that? You are certain?

LUCIUS: Just now. Her maid-in-waiting, Zara, came directly to -

PILATE: Oh-hh... None of this is to my liking.

LUCIUS: Can it be a sign, portent?..

PILATE: What to make of it? I am astounded at this Jesus. He speaks not a word in his own defence. Why, he will not even look at me. 'Stands there, centre-circle, downcast...

LUCIUS: The Jews bear him much malice.

PILATE: They are bent on blood. But why? Why the hatred?

LUCIUS: And they are playing the Roman card.

PILATE: Huh... I am loath to give in to them. And yet the more I try the more unruly they become.

LUCIUS: Eh, if I may remind you, Sir -

PILATE: What?

LUCIUS: It is the custom at the Feast for the Governor to release to the people a prisoner of their choice.

PILATE: Yes. Yes, of course -

LUCIUS: There are many felons in the dungeons. I have in mind one in particular -

PILATE: Who? Tell me -

LUCIUS: Jesus. Son of Abbas.

PILATE: Barabbas. He still lives? I found him guilty of sedition and murder. A vile creature.

LUCIUS: He is to be executed this very day. With two others.

PILATE: Come! To the point!

LUCIUS: Well, if you were to offer to release one or the other - Barabbas or the Galilean - ?

PILATE: Ah! I see what you - !

LUCIUS: We will foil the Rabbis, slip their snare -

PILATE: But of course! No one could be so malevolent as to prefer a murderer to a mute!.. I thank you, Lucius... Come, let us return to the Seat of Judgement...

THREE

PILATE: Oh, ye gods! Am I to believe my ears?! How cold! How sinisterly callous! That they should choose Barabbas, call for his release, scream instead for the execution of one in whom I can find no malice!..

LUCIUS: These people are not to blame, Sir - not the Jews.

PILATE: What?

LUCIUS: This is the work of the Sanhedrin.
The Rabbis have moved among the crowds, egging them on, whipping them into a frenzy, spurring them to call for the release of Barabbas.

PILATE: Yes. Yes, well be it so, I still -

LUCIUS: Sir, I am your commanding officer, a centurion of the Empire. I think as a military man, not as a politician. And the warrior in me says there is a mob at our gates, this garrison fortress of ours is under siege.

PILATE: So?

LUCIUS: I have a full company of militia on stand-by, at high alert. And I have positioned archers on the rooftop, at the turrets. You have but to nod, Procurator, and I will disperse this mob, lift this siege...

PILATE: Ah, but there would be bloodshed, Lucius – almost certainly - and where would it end, once begun?..
Are we to make martyrs of these fanatics?
Might not an uprising spread throughout this accursed country, precipitated at our gates?..

And once word reached Rome - as it most certainly would – how would it rebound on me?..
No. No, there is another way

LUCIUS: Sir?

PILATE: I return to the Seat of Judgment. Have a servant fetch me water and a towel.

LUCIUS: (TAKEN ABACK) But, Sir, I - ?!

PILATE: Do it. And at once!

LUCIUS: Sir...

PILATE: I will disperse this mob, lift this siege, in my own way - and without bloodshed...

FOUR

PILATE: Lucius.

LUCIUS: Sir?

PILATE: Release Barabbas. He walks - if he can walk - free.

LUCIUS: Sir. And the Galilean?

PILATE: Have him scourged. Let your militia have their way with him a while.

LUCIUS: As you wish. And then?..

PILATE: Then... if the Jews do not relent... If, if they continue to bay for blood...

LUCIUS: Sir?

PILATE: Crucify him.

FIVE

PILATE: Yes, Lucius? What is it?

LUCIUS: Sir, there is a man down in the courtyard who seeks an audience, urgently.

PILATE: Man? What man?

LUCIUS: He hails from Arimathea. By name, Joseph.

PILATE: Did he give cause for his request?

LUCIUS: Only that he has come in haste from Golgotha - and that he will detain you but briefly.

PILATE: Hmmm... From Golgotha. A Jew?

LUCIUS: A man of means, my Lord - from what I could ascertain.

PILATE: Hmmm... My bodyguard is at hand?

LUCIUS: In the corridor and at your bidding. Sir.

PILATE: Oh, very well... I will give ear to this Joseph of Arimathea...

(In the following sequence Joseph of Arimathea may be played by a third actor... or Lucius may turn away from the audience... don a cloak and/or headgear signifying Jewry... turn back to the audience to fill a different role:
nervous, hesitant, unsure of himself... but never the less firm in his resolve...)

13

SIX

PILATE: Yes?..

JOSEPH: My, my name is Jo -

PILATE: I know who you are. Come, be brief.

JOSEPH: I, I ask permission to take possession of the Nazarene's body.

PILATE: He is dead? You are certain?

JOSEPH: I was there, by the cross, when he yielded up his spirit.

PILATE: Hmmm... You were one of his followers?

JOSEPH: A silent one, alas.

PILATE: Huh... And what have you in mind should I grant your request?

JOSEPH: Why, to give him a decent burial.

PILATE: Oh?..

JOSEPH: Out beyond Golgotha I have had a tomb fashioned from the very rock -

PILATE: Yes?

JOSEPH: In, in anticipation of my own burial.

PILATE: Indeed.

JOSEPH: There I shall lay Jesus in a clean winding sheet – with your permission.

PILATE: And you will seal this tomb?

JOSEPH: There is, sir, a great rock hard by the entrance. I shall have it rolled into place once the body is -

PILATE: Then do it - with my blessing.

JOSEPH: I thank you, Governor.

PILATE: And that will be the end of it...

(PAUSE)

JOSEPH: Perhaps... Perhaps not...

(PAUSE)

PILATE: What?

JOSEPH: While he lived, sir, Jesus predicted this day – his betrayal, trial, crucifixion.

PILATE: Hmmm -

JOSEPH: He also foretold his resurrection.

PILATE: His - what?

JOSEPH: He assured his followers that within three days he would rise again - from the dead...

PILATE: Are you mad? Demented?.. You seem balanced.

JOSEPH: That was his prophesy, Sir.

PILATE: Oh, what is it about the Jews? Why can they never leave it be - be as we are?!

JOSEPH: Sir, I am merely recounting what his followers heard from his lips, will readily vouch for -

PILATE: This is preposterous!
           Look you! Jo-Joseph of, of Arimathea!
           Mark well my words:
           no one, no one - no slave, no free man -
           no Prince, no pauper,
           no King, Monarch, Emperor,
           no mortal man or woman
           of whatever race, colour, creed
           has ever, ever, come back from the dead!

JOSEPH: Sir, I -

PILATE: Yet you have the audacity - the sheer gall -
           to stand there in the fading light of day
           and assert that a Jew – a mere Jew -
           a Jew rejected and reviled by his own blood -
           a crucified Jew, to boot -
           that this, this creature - what remains of him -
           will come forth anon from the grave?!..
           Oh, ye Gods!...

JOSEPH: Indeed, Procurator, I -

PILATE: Enough of nonsense! You vex me further at your
           peril!..
           Now go! See to this, this cadaver.
           I rule the living - not the dead!..

SEVEN

LUCIUS: Sir?.. Sir!..

PILATE: Hmmm?.. What?

LUCIUS: There is a delegation in the forecourt.

PILATE: Delegation?

LUCIUS: Jews… They request a hearing.

PILATE: Request denied.

LUCIUS: Sir?

PILATE: I have had enough of Jews and Jewry for one day.

LUCIUS: As you wish, Sir.

PILATE: Eh-hhhh?..

LUCIUS: Sir?..

PILATE: Did they… signal their intent?

LUCIUS: They - they would have you mount a guard.

PILATE: What?

LUCIUS: At the tomb… where the felon's body is buried.

PILATE: Do I hear you aright?

LUCIUS: They are concerned, Sir, that -

PILATE: They want me to mount a guard? Send Roman
mercenaries to guard a tomb? A tomb?!

LUCIUS: From what I could gather, yes.

PILATE: Are they mad? Why, I would be the laughing stock of the Empire!

LUCIUS: It seems, sir, while he still lived, this fellow promised his followers -

PILATE: What!

LUCIUS: That he would come back again. From the dead. With-within three days...

PILATE: Oh-hh! This again! Three days, three days! First the elder from Arimathea, now this!

LUCIUS: They - they are apprehensive...

PILATE: Apprehensive?

LUCIUS: What if his followers return to the tomb by night, steal away the body?

PILATE: Ah-hhh...

LUCIUS: They would then be able to spread a fiction among the people Jesus is risen...

PILATE: Yes...

LUCIUS: Great harm would come of it - a disturbance perhaps, greater than the one already quelled...

PILATE: Hmmm... And their worry might well become our worry...

LUCIUS: Indeed, Sir...

PAUSE.

PILATE: Lucius.

LUCIUS: Sir?

PILATE: Go tell them the Governor of Judaea will not send men under his command to guard a grave! He will not be privy to this folly...

LUCIUS: Sir...

PILATE: Eh-hh... They have guards of their own, have they not? In their pay? On duty at the Temple?

LUCIUS: Why, yes, I -

PILATE: Then let them see to it!

PILATE: Lucius?..

LUCIUS: Sir?

PILATE: What do you make of it all?

LUCIUS: I - I...

PILATE: No, tell me. Seasoned campaigner that you are. What is your thinking?

LUCIUS: I - I do not know -

PILATE: What!

LUCIUS: I - I witnessed his death, this Jesus. He died as no felon ever would... ever could.

PILATE: Hmmm... First my wife... Now my centurion.

LUCIUS: Sir, I -

PILATE: Go back down, Lucius. Dismiss them.

LUCIUS: Sir... And if they -

PILATE: I have spoken. That is my last word…

LUCIUS: Sir…

Three days, eh? Huh… Three days from now I shall be back at base… Caesarea… Among Romans…

Sun, sea and a mellow wind, offshore…

Away from this place of superstitions and dark dissent!..

'Shaken the dust of this sinister city from my sandals – oh, so gladly!

Enough! No more pressure from the zealots - of one ilk or another!..

ENDS

Post Script

1.

"Whoever transferred Matthew's oral legacy to parchment for the first time was probably a second generation Jewish Christian who had been a disciple of the Apostle (once despised as the tax collector, Levi, until he was called by Jesus). (Mt. 9.9; Mark 2.14; Luke 5.27.)

This version of the Good News was formulated about 85 A.D., perhaps a little later, among the Jewish and Gentile Christians at Antioch in Syria - where Matthew's community of converts reputedly took root and where *his oral legacy may very well have become his written gospel...*

The evangelist was writing to and for his fellow Jewish Christians, many of them under pressure from their fellow Jews, verbal and physical, to renounce the new religion, return to Orthodoxy. And they had begun to waver - hence this testament.

They were in need of assurance that Jesus was the fulfillment of the Law and the prophets; re-assurance that in living the gospel they were remaining true to their Jewish roots...

2.

A drama/dramas set against the backdrop of the first Good Friday in which the Central persona is neither seen nor heard – but whose words and deeds are constantly referred to...

The idea really began to germinate back in the sixties when I was a visitor in the Big Apple. I found Greenwich Village - as it was then - quite fascinating. There I saw Theatre-in-the-Round for the very first time - I was amazed...

Then one evening I went to a cinema quite off Broadway to see a film, The Gospel According to Matthew, directed by a young, relatively unknown Italian, Pier Paulo Pasolini. In black and white. Stark, barren landscapes. A cast of extras, no big names, no stars. So different from the Hollywood treatment of the Christ story. I was blown away...

I emerged from that cinema into a humid New York night. And the thought came to me - why not The Passion according to Matthew? That was the start of a long road.

3.

An earlier draft ended with Pilate's sudden dismissal of Joseph of Arimathea:

- Enough! You vex me further at your peril! Now go - see to this cadaver! I rule the living - not the dead!..

Crescendo, yes. But more than a whit abruptly. The audience was thrown, they needed more, wanted a smoother landing... I began to mull, as is my wont...

4.

In June, a few years back, my wife and I spent a few days in Paris. I wanted to view the Rembrant exhibition in the Louvre "Rembrant et la figure du Christ." I was fascinated by the various sketches the Master made as he tried one thing, then another, searching for a real-life portrait of Jesus. (These were mounted on the walls of the exhibition area.)

Fascinated, too, by his modus agendi it seems he recruited one Jew after another from among the local population in his home town, had them back to his apartment, sit for him while he sketched...

And so to the original, the finished work, a portrait of Christ like no other before... A true original that spurned the unreal images of the Middle Ages and the Renaissance... I could only stand in awe and wonderment.

The next morning I rose early, made tea, sat at the table by the window, reached for paper and pen... That exhibition had triggered something in me and within the hour I had completed the first draft of what was to become - several drafts later - the final scene:

Pilate rises, turns to Lucius, incredulous:

- Do I hear you aright? They want me to send soldiers under my command to guard a tomb? A tomb! Why, I would be the laughing stock of the Empire!.. Go tell them, the Governor of Judaea will not be privy to this folly!..

Eh-hhh... They have guards of their own, have they not, mercenaries in their pay? Well, then, let them see to it...

There you have it! Guards from the Temple, loyal to the High Priest, on the Sanhedrin payroll, guarded the Tomb – not Roman soldiers loyal to Pilate.

Why the emphasis?

Matthew's Passion narrative begins with a bribe (Judas) and ends with a bribe – much easier for Caiaphas and his Inner Circle to bribe their own guards than soldiers loyal to Rome. And make it stick...

Sean Walsh

His plays have been broadcast on RTE, BBC and – in translation - on European networks; televised on RTE, BBC One and Channel 4; staged at the Abbey National theatre (the Peacock, studio space), the Project Arts, the London fringe and the Liverpool Playhouse.

Credits include *The Dreamers, Earwig, The Search for Xavier, Assault on a Citadel, Centre Circle, Fugitive, Far Side of the Moon, Notes on the Past Imperfect, Veil, Pilate Under Pressure, The Night of the Rouser, 125 Valium Valley, Dead Man Talking, Travels with my Dad, Jenny One Two Three.*

A number of his scripts published on Amazon... paperback and Kindle. Also Smashwords.com

Website www.sean-walsh.me

The final performance of Pilate Under Pressure 1

Applause! Well deserved... Gardiner street Jesuit Church, Dublin... the final performance of Pilate Under Pressure 1... A few days later a woman, a stranger, stopped me on the street: "Thank you for your play. It was so different..."

"His habit, Father – Xavier's habit
is hanging on the back of his door..."

THE SEARCH FOR XAVIER

SEAN WALSH

"Once he signs it he's out – gone... forever... That's what it says in
the document – sine spei reddiendi... without any hope of return..."

"If we try to cover up we'll be denying Xavier... What?..
The prayers of the Faithful... the intercession of the People of God..."

JENNY

Just when I was beginning to get the hang of Jenny One, she disappeared. Enter Jenny Two... Oh, oh.

ONE

SEAN WALSH

TWO

Is there life after Jenny Two?.. Yes! Oh, yes!.. Welcome, Jenny Three!

THREE

"And for all our rows and falling-outs, I loved you, Dad, and always will, no matter what. Don't ask me to explain, I couldn't.

It's what I feel, not what I know..."

BEHIND CLOSED DOORS
AT THE HOUSE OF THE HIGH PRIEST

CONCLAVE

SEAN WALSH

"Oh, my Rabbis! I say it with all the wisdom of your High Priest -
better that one man die than the entire nation perish..." - Caiaphas.

"And but now one of the Twelve has offered to betray him with a kiss for a mere thirty pieces of silver – the price of a slave! Will anyone tell me this Jesus is the Messiah?"

Set against the backdrop
of the first Good Friday

VEIL

*"There is someone - something - in there
but it is not our Misach..."*

"Who are you?
We are – the Cold..."

SEAN WALSH

"He speaks – but not with the voice of my son-
We speak with many voices – we are many..."

"Don't you see? I just can't stand here while he's being led out to...
I must go to him, I must!

Veronica!.. Take your veil..."

Heaney on Veil.

Department of English, Queen's University, Belfast. 1966.

The idea of approaching the significance of the Passion obliquely, through the experiences of those who might be regarded as enemies, is good theatre; and the actual denouement is all the more dramatic for not taking place in the presence of the Saviour.

In fact, the reality of the Incarnation seems to me properly realised in the movement - Christ's life becomes dynamic and efficacious in the world...

The devil's part, as ever in literature, comes off best here, I think...

In the main, the speech is attractively dignified and in character. And I think that Misach's outbreak in the end is the most exciting thing in the play, both as a dramatic device and as speech - after long silence.

Misach, incidentally, would be my nominee for the best dramatic figure in the cast. Definitely a step well beyond the weeping women and the cowering apostles.

I was kept reading, which is the most important thing in the end...

- Seamus Heaney.

(At the time I knew little enough about Seamus Heaney - and he certainly knew nothing about me!)

VEIL was staged and published several years before THE EXORCIST stormed America... went on to make millions at the box office... VEIL made buttons.

Sean Walsh

Notes On The Past Imperfect

"Long walk down a short corridor into a circle of strangers. Emma across from me, my wayward wife… Strangest of them all…"

50230647R00020